GUINEA PIG GANG

Books in the Animal Ark Pets series

1 Puppy Puzzle
2 Kitten Crowd
3 Rabbit Race
4 Hamster Hotel
5 Mouse Magic
6 Chick Challenge
7 Pony Parade
8 Guinea Pig Gang

Ben M. Baglio

GUINEA PIG GANG

Illustrated by
Paul Howard

Cover illustration by
Chris Chapman

A
LITTLE APPLE
PAPERBACK

SCHOLASTIC INC.
New York Toronto London Auckland Sydney

Special thanks to Helen Magee.
Thanks also to C. J. Hall, B.Vet.Med., M.R.C.V.S., for reviewing
the veterinary material contained in this book.

ISBN 0-590-18748-1

12 11 10 9 8 7 6 5 4 3 2 1   8 9/9 0 1 2 3/0

Printed in the U.S.A.   40
First Scholastic printing, February 1998

Contents

1. Pet Day at School   1
2. Carla the Cavy   14
3. Guinea Pigs Galore   24
4. Carla in Trouble   41
5. A Good Idea!   54
6. Carla's New Home   62
7. Bad News   76
8. The Welford Show   85

GUINEA PIG GANG

1

Pet Day at School

"Oh, Pam, you *are* lucky to have such a beautiful pet!" said Mandy Hope. She gazed at the reddish-brown guinea pig, scampering around the classroom floor. "You are adorable, Ginny!"

Ginny, the guinea pig, was surrounded by a wide ring of children, sitting cross-legged on the floor. Every so often she would scurry up to one of them, twitching her whiskers and snuffling.

"You think *all* animals are adorable," James Hunter said to Mandy. His eyes were shining behind his glasses.

"And *you* like animals almost as much as Mandy does," said Pam Stanton to James.

Mandy and James grinned at Pam. Mandy's parents were both vets in the little village of Welford. Their clinic was called Animal Ark and it was at the back of their stone cottage.

There were always a lot of animals coming in and out of Animal Ark. Mandy loved it. Mandy thought animals were the most important things in the world. James was her best friend. He had a black Labrador named Blackie.

Ginny ran across the floor and stopped in front of a girl with short red-brown hair.

"She likes you, Lisa," Pam said as Ginny sat back on her haunches and looked at Lisa with her bright button eyes.

Lisa Glover was in James's class. She stretched

out a hand gently. The little guinea pig sniffed at it, then put one tiny paw into Lisa's palm. She lifted Ginny up and stroked her fur.

"Lisa thinks Ginny is adorable, too," said James.

Mandy smiled. "Look!" she said. "Lisa's hair is almost the same color as Ginny's coat."

Lisa looked up at Mrs. Todd and Mrs. Black. The two teachers had organized a pet afternoon every Friday. "This is the best Pet Day yet," she said to them. "I love guinea pigs."

"I think we've had a very successful session," Mrs. Todd agreed. "Ginny has been very well-behaved and I'm sure we're all very grateful to Pam for all the information she's given us." Mrs. Todd was Mandy's teacher at Welford Village School.

Lisa walked across to Pam and held Ginny out to her. Pam took Ginny in her arms and gave her a cuddle.

"Stay where you are until Pam has put Ginny in her cage," Mrs. Todd said. "We don't want our guinea pig guest to get frightened."

"Let's hope your projects are as successful as Pam's talk," Mrs. Black joked. "And I hope everyone is going to enter their pets for the best-kept pet competition at the Welford Show. We certainly seem to have a lot of expert pet owners here in Welford."

James was in the class below Mandy at school. Mrs. Black, his teacher, often joined up with Mrs. Todd for projects. Each week of that term one of the pupils would bring in their pet and explain how to look after it. Lots of them had already decided to enter their pets in the Welford Show, which took place once a year.

"This is a great way to spend Friday afternoons," Mandy said, tickling Ginny under the chin. "I'm going to do a drawing of Ginny for the project."

"And I'll do a food chart for her," James added.

"I'll help you," Gary Roberts said.

"And me," Jill Redfern offered.

The two classes buzzed with excitement as they planned their projects. Pam put Ginny back in her cage and the little animal began grooming herself. Ginny had a smooth reddish-brown coat and bright black eyes.

"Guinea pigs keep themselves really clean, don't they?" Richard Tanner said. "Just like cats." Richard had a Persian cat called Duchess.

Pam nodded. "You don't have to bathe them," she said. "But sometimes I brush Ginny's coat just because I like doing it — and Ginny likes it, too."

James had started a list. "I've put down

crushed oats and guinea pig mixture," he said. "What else does Ginny eat, Pam?"

"She needs lots of greens and roots," Pam said. "And don't forget hay and water."

"Hay?" asked Peter Foster.

Pam nodded. "Guinea pigs love it," she said. "A handful or two each day should be enough. If there's any left over the guinea pig will use it for bedding. You have to make sure there aren't any thistles in it, though. They can hurt the guinea pig's throat."

"That's a lot to remember," Amy Tenton said.

"You get used to it," Pam said. "*You* don't forget how to look after Minnie, *do* you?"

Amy shook her head. "Oh, no," she said. "I couldn't do that." Minnie was Amy's white mouse.

"It seems to me you all look after your pets very well," Mrs. Todd said. "I can't imagine Peter forgetting to give Timmy his dinner."

Peter grinned. "Timmy would remind me!" he said. Timmy was a cairn terrier and the naughtiest dog in Welford.

"Whose turn is it next week?" Mrs. Black asked.

"Mine," said Jill. "I'm bringing Toto." Toto was Jill's tortoise.

"Who wants to do the session after that?" asked Mrs. Todd.

A bunch of hands shot up into the air.

"Can I bring Gertie?" Gary asked.

"I could bring Blackie," said James.

"Let's have Blackie that week and Gertie the

garter snake the week after," Mrs. Black suggested.

James grinned with pride.

Gary was pleased, too. "Great," he said. "I'm going to read as much as I can about snakes before then."

"Who else has a pet?" asked Mrs. Todd. "We want all of your pets to visit us."

"What about you, Lisa?" Mrs. Black asked.

Lisa blushed. "I don't have a pet," she said.

"Oh, too bad," said Sarah Drummond. "You should get a puppy. James and I have both got black Labradors. We got them from the same litter."

"Mine is called Blackie," said James.

"And mine is Licorice," said Sarah. "He's gorgeous."

Lisa bit her lip. "I mean I don't have a pet *yet*," she said. "In fact I'm getting a guinea pig next week."

Pam smiled widely. "A guinea pig!" she said. "That's terrific. What kind?"

"Oh, a really special one," Lisa said. "It's

called a tort and white. It's got black, white, and red markings. It isn't just an ordinary guinea pig."

Pam looked at Ginny. "I don't think *Ginny* is ordinary either," she said.

"But this is a cavy," said Lisa.

"What's that?" James asked.

"It's a pedigree guinea pig," Lisa answered. "A purebred."

"Lots of people in school have guinea pigs," Jill said.

"That's right," said Pam. "We've even got a Guinea Pig Gang. There are five of us. We all have guinea pigs and we meet up every week with our pets to play with them and talk about them. You can join if you want."

"You can bring your guinea pig to school and let us see it," said Mandy.

"And you can bring it to visit Ginny," added Pam.

Lisa blushed even more. "Oh, no," she said. "I couldn't do that. I wouldn't be allowed to. It's a *pedigree*."

The bell for the end of school rang and Lisa turned away.

"Well," said Pam. "It looks like Ginny isn't good enough to mix with a *pedigree* guinea pig!"

"She didn't mean it like that," Mandy said.

Pam snorted. "I think Lisa Glover is really snobby," she said. "A guinea pig doesn't have to be a pedigree to be beautiful."

Pam picked up Ginny's cage and walked toward the classroom door.

"Uh-oh!" said James. "Pam is really upset. Lisa shouldn't have said that."

Mandy frowned. "I think Lisa was upset, too," she said.

"What about?" James asked.

"I don't know," she said. "But I got the feeling she was unhappy about something."

"She wasn't very nice to Pam about Ginny," James replied.

Mandy shook her head. "But Lisa *loved* Ginny," she said. "Didn't you see the way she

held her? And she was really interested in everything Pam was saying about looking after guinea pigs."

"So why was she so snobby about her pedigree guinea pig?" said James.

Mandy frowned. "I'm not sure," she said. "But I know one thing. Lisa didn't care about Ginny not being a pedigree. She really liked her."

"Mmm," said James. "Well, I thought she

was snobby." He grinned. "Are you coming to my house tonight? I've taught Blackie a new trick and I want you to see it. He loves showing off."

Mandy laughed. "Don't tell me," she said. "He can sit still for two minutes!"

"No," said James. "I don't think Blackie will ever be able to do that. But he can beg for a biscuit. You should see him catch it."

"Are you going to put him in the Welford Show?" asked Mandy. "There's a really big pet section this year."

James shook his head. "Not this time," he said. "But maybe next year — if I can get him to walk, to heel, to sit, and to come when called."

"Grandma is going to have a home-baking booth at the show," Mandy added.

"Is she going to make cookies for it?" James asked.

"And doughnuts."

"Do you think your grandma would let me help on the booth?" said James.

"Only if you promised not to eat all the cookies," Mandy replied. "Now, what are you going to say at the pets session?"

Mandy and James discussed James's talk all the way home. But at the back of her mind Mandy was still wondering what it was that had upset Lisa.

2

Carla the Cavy

"Guess what?" Mandy said as she came into the kitchen of Animal Ark the following Wednesday after school.

"You put your backpack away instead of leaving it in the hall for me to trip over," Dr. Adam Hope replied, his dark eyes twinkling.

Mandy grinned. "Nope!" she said. "Some-

14

thing much more exciting than that. Do you give up?"

Dr. Adam and Dr. Emily Hope nodded.

"Lisa Glover has got her guinea pig," Mandy said, plonking herself down at the table.

"The tort and white?" said Dr. Adam. "They're very unusual. I'd love to see it."

"I knew you would," said Mandy. "So I told her she could bring it here tonight for a check-up. Is that all right?"

Dr. Adam laughed. "Ask your mom," he said. "She's the one doing evening clinic hours."

Dr. Emily shook her head. She had bright-red hair tied in a ponytail. "Mandy, you should have checked with Jean." Jean Knox was Animal Ark's receptionist.

"Oh, you aren't all booked up, are you?" asked Mandy. "I thought it would be okay."

Dr. Emily shook her head again. "I suppose I can squeeze in another appointment," she said. "But in the future ask your friends to go through Jean."

"I will," said Mandy. Then she looked worried. "What if it's an emergency?"

"An emergency is different," Dr. Adam said. "We'll always see an animal in an emergency. There isn't anything wrong with the guinea pig, is there?" asked Dr. Adam.

Mandy shook her head. "No, but Lisa's mom thought it should have a checkup."

"Very wise," said Dr. Emily. She looked at Mandy. "And the answer is yes — as long as you don't get in the way."

"Yes, what?" asked Mandy, puzzled.

"Yes, you *can* come into the clinic while I examine the guinea pig," said Dr. Emily.

"Yippee!" said Mandy. "That's great, Mom."

Lisa and her sister, Jennifer, brought the guinea pig into the clinic that evening in a brand-new cage. Jennifer was thirteen, five years older than Lisa. The sisters weren't at all alike. Lisa had short reddish-brown hair and dark eyes. Jennifer had long blonde hair and blue eyes. Nobody would ever guess they were sisters.

Mandy looked eagerly at the little guinea pig. She drew in her breath in surprise. She had *never* seen a guinea pig like it before!

"This is Carla," Jennifer said, putting the cage down on the examination table.

"Oh, she's gorgeous," Mandy said. "Just look at her markings, Mom!"

"She's a tortoiseshell and white," Jennifer said.

"That's quite a big name for a little animal," Dr. Emily said, smiling.

The guinea pig was marked with square patches of red, black, and white. Looked at from above, she looked like she was wearing a checkered coat.

"She really is beautiful," Dr. Emily said. "Tort and whites are so difficult to breed. You've got a very good specimen here, Lisa."

"They *are* difficult to breed," Jennifer agreed. "That's why they're so special and *that's* why I wanted her."

Mandy looked curiously at Jennifer and Lisa. Lisa hadn't said a word. Jennifer was acting as if

Carla was *her* guinea pig. Maybe Carla was a family pet — not just Lisa's.

"She's very healthy as well," Dr. Emily said, putting Carla back in her cage. "You shouldn't have any problems there at all."

"Thanks, Dr. Emily," Lisa said. "I'm glad you like her."

"Nobody could help liking her," Dr. Emily said. "She's a beauty."

Jennifer nodded as Dr. Emily went to the sink to wash her hands. "Of course she is," she said. "She's a prizewinner."

The three girls trooped out of the clinic.

"Has Carla won prizes?" Mandy asked, surprised.

"Not yet," said Jennifer. "But she will. The Welford Show is at the end of next month. There's a guinea pig competition this year. I'm going to put Carla in the purebred section — that's for pedigree guinea pigs. She's bound to win a prize."

"*You* are?" asked Mandy. "But I thought Carla was Lisa's guinea pig."

Jennifer looked at her little sister. "Oh, no," she said. "Carla is mine. She was a birthday present. And I've told Lisa she can't mess around with her."

"I only want to play with her," Lisa explained.

"Well, you can't," said Jennifer. "She's mine. And I don't want her all fussed over. She's got to look her best for the show if she's going to win a prize."

"Guinea pigs like company," Mandy said carefully to Jennifer. "They don't mind being fussed over. They enjoy it."

Jennifer looked down her nose at Mandy. "You're only a year older than Lisa," she said. "What do *you* know?"

"Mandy knows lots about animals," Lisa said. "She knows more than you do."

Mandy looked at Lisa in surprise and Lisa blushed.

"Just because her parents are vets doesn't mean she knows everything," Jennifer said.

"Of course not," said Mandy. "I don't know

all that much about animals. But I do like
them."

"Are you saying I don't?" asked Jennifer,
tossing her hair back. "I think Carla is beautiful. That's why I wanted her for my birthday.
Nobody else I know has got such a pretty pet."

Jennifer turned around and marched off.
Mandy looked at Lisa.

"Sorry about Jennifer," Lisa said to Mandy.
"Ever since she turned thirteen she thinks she's
all grown up and I'm just a little kid."

"It's really a shame that she won't let you play with Carla," Mandy said. "Guinea pigs really *love* being played with."

"I know," said Lisa. "But Jennifer won't listen. She doesn't know the first thing about guinea pigs and she won't let me touch Carla. She only wanted Carla because she thought she looked beautiful. But that isn't right. You can't have a pet just because you think it looks beautiful."

Mandy bit her lip. Lisa was really upset.

"Once Jennifer gets to know Carla she'll like her for all sorts of reasons," Mandy said. "Not just because she looks beautiful."

"I hope so," said Lisa. "Do you know that she couldn't make up her mind whether she wanted a stereo or a guinea pig for her birthday?"

"But she *did* choose to have a guinea pig," said Mandy.

"Only because Carla was so special," Lisa said. "If *I* had one I wouldn't care if it was a pedigree or not."

Jennifer's voice floated back to them. "Come on, Lisa!" she called.

Lisa gave Mandy a quick smile and turned to go. "See you," she said.

Mandy watched as she walked off after her sister.

Poor Lisa. Imagine having an animal at home and not even being allowed to play with it. No wonder she was unhappy!

3

Guinea Pigs Galore

Next day at school, Mandy told Pam all about Jennifer and Carla.

"People like Jennifer shouldn't be allowed to have pets," Pam said.

Mandy shook her head. "I don't think Jennifer *means* to be unkind to Carla. It's just that she doesn't know anything about guinea pigs."

"She should have been in our class last Friday," James said. "Then she would know all about them. You were really good, Pam."

Pam blushed. "Thanks," she replied. "But I can't understand why Jennifer would even want a guinea pig when she doesn't want to find out about them."

"She wanted Carla because she's so unusual," Mandy explained.

"She's beautiful," James agreed. "I've never seen a guinea pig like that before."

"Perfect," Mandy added. Then she frowned. "It's just that her owner isn't."

"Shh!" said James. "Here comes Lisa."

They turned as Lisa came through the school gates. She was walking with her head down, scuffing her feet.

"Hi, Lisa!" Mandy said. "What's up?"

Lisa shrugged. "Nothing really," she said. "By the way, thanks for trying to talk to Jennifer yesterday."

"I don't suppose she's changed her mind about letting you play with Carla," Mandy said.

Lisa shook her head. "I wouldn't mind if Jennifer played with her. But she doesn't. Poor Carla is getting so bored."

"That isn't *your* fault," James said. "You *want* to play with her. It's Jennifer that says you can't."

"That's wrong," said Mandy. "Pets aren't possessions."

"Try telling that to Jennifer," Lisa said.

Pam put her head to one side. "How would you like to come and visit Ginny?" she asked.

Lisa's face lit up. "Could I?" she said. "That would be great."

"Ginny would love it," Pam said. "Come on Friday after school. That's when the Guinea Pig Gang meets."

"You told me about that before," said Lisa. "Who's in it?"

"There are five of us," Pam said. "Robbie Taylor, Kate Fletcher, Ross Jarvis, Zoe Adams, and me. We all have guinea pigs and we take turns meeting at each other's house once a week. The guinea pigs really enjoy it. So do we. It's my turn this week."

"I'd love to come," said Lisa. "Thanks, Pam."

"You two could come, too," Pam said to Mandy and James.

"But we don't have guinea pigs," said Mandy.

Pam laughed. "Oh, that's all right," she said. "You can be honorary members!"

The bell rang for the start of school and they made their way toward their classes. Lisa and Pam were chatting about the Guinea Pig Gang.

"Lisa looks a lot happier now," James said to Mandy.

Mandy smiled. "I think Pam's Guinea Pig Gang will really cheer her up," she said. "And me, too! I'm really looking forward to Friday. Jill is doing her talk about Toto *and* we're going to see the Guinea Pig Gang."

Mandy and James were still talking about Toto the tortoise when they arrived at Pam's house.

"Imagine hibernating all winter," James said. "I think I'd rather have a year-round pet like Blackie."

Lisa came running down the road. They waited for her and walked up the front path together.

"Hi," said Pam, opening the door. "Come and see the guinea pigs."

They went through the house and out into the backyard. Ross, Robbie, Zoe, and Kate were there already with their guinea pigs. The pets were scampering around in two big cardboard boxes.

"Why have you got two boxes?" James asked.

"Because we don't want to have any baby guinea pigs," Pam said. She pointed at one box. "These are the boys — Micky and Scamp."

"And these are the girls — Ginny, Brownie, and Muffin," said Ross.

"Oh, they're so cute!" said Lisa, kneeling down to watch the guinea pigs. "Look at them playing."

Ross had a short-haired black guinea pig called Micky. Zoe's and Kate's were both rough-haired crossbreeds and Robbie's was a long-haired tan-colored boar.

"That's Scamp," Robbie said.

"He looks adorable," Lisa said. "But he must be a lot of work with that long coat."

Robbie grinned. "I have to brush him every day," he said. "His coat gets tangled if I don't. But I don't mind. I like grooming him."

Lisa put out her hand and stroked Scamp's coat. "What do you use?" she asked.

"An ordinary hairbrush," Robbie said. "But

sometimes, if his coat gets really tangled, I have to snip the knots out."

"I use a baby hairbrush to groom Muffin," Zoe said.

Pam picked up Ginny and gave her a cuddle. She seemed worried.

"Is Ginny all right?" Kate asked.

Pam frowned. "I don't know," she said. "She looks okay, but she isn't running around as much as usual."

"She *does* seem a little tired," Mandy said to Pam.

Pam nodded. "She was all right this morning," she replied. "But she didn't eat very well yesterday. I'm worried about her. She's usually running around."

"Why don't you bring her to Animal Ark?" Mandy suggested. "You could call for an appointment."

Pam nodded. "I'll bring her tomorrow if she isn't any better," she said. "It isn't like Ginny not to want to eat."

"Hey, look at Muffin and Brownie!" Ross said.

They all looked. The two guinea pigs were circling each other and making little darting movements.

"They look as if they're dancing," James said, laughing.

"Is there a guinea pig dancing competition at the Welford Show?" Zoe asked. "We could enter them for it!"

"I thought I might enter Scamp in the guinea pig competition," Robbie said. "*If* I can keep his coat untangled," he added.

Everybody started talking about the Welford Show, but Mandy noticed that Pam kept looking at Ginny. She was obviously very worried.

Ginny wasn't better on Saturday morning. The phone rang at Animal Ark as Mandy was helping her mom clear the breakfast dishes.

"That was Pam Stanton," Dr. Adam explained, poking his head in the kitchen door. "She's bringing Ginny over in half an hour."

Mandy put a pile of plates on the draining board. "Is Ginny worse?" she asked.

"She's still not eating," said Dr. Adam.

"I hope it isn't anything serious," Mandy said.

Dr. Emily smiled at her. "Don't be too worried," she said. "She probably only needs her teeth clipped. Sometimes guinea pigs' teeth grow too long to let them eat properly."

But Mandy couldn't help worrying when she knew an animal was unwell.

It seemed like ages before Pam and her mother arrived with Ginny.

"Well, well, what have we here?" Dr. Adam said, as he lifted the little animal out of her cage.

Simon, the nurse, laid a fresh sheet of paper on the examination table and Dr. Adam put Ginny down on it.

Mandy and Pam watched anxiously. Dr.

Adam felt Ginny's throat gently, then put his thumbs on either side of her jaw. The guinea pig opened her mouth.

"What's wrong with her?" asked Mrs. Stanton.

"Is it serious?" Pam added, looking worried.

Dr. Adam looked at Pam and smiled. "I don't think it's too serious," he said. "Her teeth are all right, but her throat seems to be quite painful. I'm not surprised she hasn't been eating."

"What are you going to do, Dad?" Mandy asked.

Dr. Adam settled Ginny in one hand and stroked her with the other.

"First I'm going to have to give her some anesthesia," he said. He looked at Mrs. Stanton. "I'll need your permission. You'll have to sign a consent form."

"Anything you say," Mrs. Stanton said. "Does she need an operation?"

Dr. Adam nodded. "Just a tiny one," he said. "It looks as if she's got an abscess in her throat."

"Then we'd better take care of it," Mrs. Stanton said.

"Jean will give you the form," Dr. Adam explained.

Mrs. Stanton nodded. "You do what you have to do," she said. "I know Ginny will be safe with you."

"How would Ginny get an abscess?" asked Mandy, as Mrs. Stanton went out.

"Mostly it's caused by thistles in the hay," Dr. Adam said. "You have to be really careful to clean out any thistles before you put the hay in the cage."

"But I'm always careful," said Pam, her face pale. "I must have missed one. Oh, poor Ginny. Can you help her?"

"It doesn't look too bad," said Dr. Adam. "But you two girls will have to wait outside."

Mandy bit her lip. Waiting was always the difficult part.

"Come on," said Simon. "The sooner we get started the sooner it'll be over."

Mandy and Pam went out into the waiting

room. Pam looked back nervously as Simon shut the door behind them.

"Now, don't worry so much, Pam," Mrs. Stanton said. She was standing at Jean's desk. There was an official–looking form in front of her.

"I can't help it," Pam said.

"Why don't you go and have something to drink while your mom and I do the paper-work?" Jean Knox suggested.

Mandy smiled at her. "Good idea, Jean," she said. "Will you call us when Dad has finished?"

Jean nodded. Her glasses fell off her nose and bounced at the end of their chain. "I'll let you know as soon as I hear anything," she said.

Mandy led Pam through to the kitchen.

"Don't worry," she said as she poured out two glasses of juice. "Dad will make Ginny better."

Pam looked at her. "I can't help it," she said. "If anything happened to Ginny I don't know what I'd do. And it's my fault. I must have left a thistle in her hay."

"Anybody could do that," said Mandy.

Pam shook her head. "And to think I was saying things about Lisa's sister," she said. "*I* can't even look after Ginny."

"That isn't true," said Mandy. "No pet could have a better owner."

Pam looked at her. "Do you really think so?" she asked.

Mandy nodded. "I think you should enter Ginny in the guinea pig competition at the Welford Show," she said. "I'm sure she'll win."

"If she gets better," said Pam.

"*When* she gets better," Mandy said firmly.

Pam smiled. "Thanks, Mandy," she said. "It really helps having you here waiting with me."

It was about ten minutes later when Jean put her head around the kitchen door. Mrs. Stanton was behind her.

"Do you want to see the patient?" Jean asked.

Mandy and Pam jumped off their chairs and dashed through the door. "Is she all right?" Pam asked.

Jean beamed. "All better, according to Simon," she said. "But she's still a little drowsy."

"You go first, Pam," Mrs. Stanton said.

The girls pushed the clinic door open and Pam went to the examination table. Ginny looked very small and sleepy.

"Can I pick her up?" asked Pam.

Dr. Adam nodded. "Just don't touch her neck or throat," he said. "She'll be a bit tender for a day or two. But she's a fine, healthy guinea pig."

"So she'll get better?" said Pam.

Simon grinned. "Of course she will," he said. "She's fit and strong. She's been very well looked after."

Pam cuddled Ginny very gently. "I'm so relieved," she said.

"I want to keep her here overnight," said Dr. Adam. "But she can go back home tomorrow. Just make sure she gets plenty of tender loving care."

"Oh, I will," said Pam. "I'll watch out for thistles from now on."

"What about the show?" said Mandy. "Are you going to enter her in the guinea pig competition? If I were a judge I'd vote for her."

"Then I will," said Pam. "And I'll make sure she's the best-kept guinea pig in the whole world!"

4

Carla in Trouble

Pam came to pick up Ginny on Sunday.

"Remember, no thistles," Dr. Adam said as he handed the little animal over.

Pam put Ginny gently in her cage. "I promise," she said. "I've told the rest of the Guinea Pig Gang that they have to be careful, too."

"Good for you," said Dr. Adam.

"Do you think Jennifer would join the Guinea Pig Gang?" Mandy asked Pam.

Pam shook her head. "I think Jennifer would think she was too grown-up," she said. "But we could ask Lisa to mention it to her."

"Let's do that," said Mandy. "We'll ask her at school tomorrow."

But when Mandy and James mentioned the idea, Lisa shook her head. "I've already told her about the Guinea Pig Gang," she said. "Jennifer says that's just for kids and their pets — not for pedigree guinea pigs."

"But Carla is a pet, too," said James.

"Jennifer only cares about her winning a prize at the show," said Lisa. "She's already started moaning about having to look after Carla and what a lot of work it is."

"Won't she let you help?" asked Mandy.

Lisa shook her head. "She won't let me near her," she said. "And I'm getting really worried. Carla's moping and she isn't looking nearly as healthy as she did when Jennifer got her. She certainly isn't going to be at her best for the show."

"Jennifer won't like that," said James.

"If Carla doesn't win a prize Jennifer won't want her at *all,*" said Lisa.

Mandy bit her lip. "We've got to do something about this," she said.

"But what?" asked James. "Carla is Jennifer's guinea pig."

Mandy frowned. "I'm beginning to think Pam was right," she said. "I don't think Jennifer should have a guinea pig if she won't look after it."

"I'll try talking to her again," said Lisa. "Not that she ever listens to me — but I'll try."

Mandy and James were very busy for the rest of the week. James rehearsed his talk every day and Mandy tried to get Blackie to sit while James spoke. But every time the Labrador heard his name he jumped up, wagging his tail in delight.

"Try to do the talk without saying that

word," said Mandy on the way to school on Friday afternoon.

"What word?" said James.

"Blackie," Mandy said.

Blackie gave a short bark and jumped up, licking Mandy's face.

Mandy burst out laughing. "It's no good, James," she said. "You'll just have to explain to everyone that Blackie is a very energetic dog."

"Lively," said James, grinning.

"Full of fun," Mandy agreed.

"Disobedient," James said regretfully.

Mandy didn't hear. "Look!" she said. "There's Lisa. She's upset about something."

Lisa was standing by the school gates, waiting for Mandy and James. She looked close to tears.

"What's the matter?" Mandy asked.

"Mom says Jennifer has to get rid of Carla," Lisa said.

"What?" said Mandy.

"But why?" James asked.

Blackie nudged Lisa's hand with his nose and she knelt down and put her arms around his neck.

"My mom says Jennifer isn't looking after Carla," she went on. "And she's right. Poor little Carla. Her fur has started to come out and she's scratching badly. Jennifer says she won't be fit to enter the Welford Show."

"So what is she going to do with her?" Mandy asked, horrified.

"Mom says we have to bring Carla into An-

imal Ark," Lisa said. "Honestly, you should see her. She looks terrible."

"Bring her tonight," Mandy said. "If you get there early enough Mom or Dad will be able to see Carla right away."

"But we don't have an appointment," said Lisa.

Mandy set her lips in a firm line. "That doesn't matter," she said. "This sounds like an emergency!"

Mandy could hardly think about anything else all afternoon. Even James's talk didn't take her mind off Carla's problems.

"That was very good, James," Mrs. Todd said when he had finished. "Blackie is such a charmer. He's full of fun."

James smiled and looked at Mandy.

"That's what we think," he said.

Mandy smiled back at him, but she was anxious to get home to tell her parents about Carla.

"You were terrific," she said to James.

James nodded. "But you're thinking about Carla, aren't you?" he said. "So am I."

Mandy smiled bigger this time. That was one of the good things about James. He always understood how worried she got when an animal was in trouble.

Jennifer and Lisa came to Animal Ark just before the clinic closed.

"I'm certainly glad you brought Carla in," Dr. Emily said after she had examined the guinea pig.

Mandy looked at poor Carla. Her beautiful check coat was sticking up in tufts and she had big bare patches all over her.

"What is the matter with her?" Jennifer asked.

Dr. Emily smiled. "Nothing too bad," she said. "She's got mites. It looks a lot worse than it actually is."

"What are mites?" Lisa asked.

"They're tiny little creatures that burrow under a guinea pig's skin," Dr. Emily said. "They must be making poor Carla very itchy. That's why she's scratching so much and losing her fur."

"Ugh!" said Jennifer. "Mites! That's horrible."

"It certainly is — for Carla," Dr. Emily said gently.

Jennifer went a bit red. "Look, Dr. Emily," she said, "I don't really think I want a guinea pig anymore. I didn't realize how much *work* it would be. Mom says I should try and find Carla another home. Can you help?"

"But you can't just give Carla away," Lisa said to Jennifer.

"She's my guinea pig, not yours," Jennifer replied.

Dr. Emily looked down at Carla. Mandy held her breath. What was going to happen?

"Why don't you leave her here at Animal Ark with us until we get rid of the mites?" Dr. Emily said. "Then we can think about what to do with her."

"All right," said Jennifer. "Only, don't ask me to touch her. Mites! Yuck!"

Dr. Emily looked at Mandy and Lisa. They were trying really hard not to say anything to Jennifer.

"Maybe taking care of pets isn't your thing," Dr. Emily said to Jennifer.

Jennifer took a step back from poor, scruffy-looking Carla. "I think you're right," she said. "And Mom thinks so, too." She sighed. "I wish I'd got a stereo for my birthday instead of a guinea pig. It would be a lot less trouble. Still, if you could help find a home for her that would be all right."

"Won't you miss her?" Lisa asked Jennifer.

Jennifer wrinkled her nose. "I won't miss all that cleaning out and stuff," she said. "Pets are a lot of work."

"But you could try to like it for Carla's sake," Lisa pleaded. "Can't you try just one more time?"

Jennifer shook her head. "I guess I'm just not

49

a pet person," she said. She looked at Carla "Mites! Carla will never win a prize looking like that."

Lisa and Mandy looked at each other. There were tears in Lisa's eyes, but Jennifer didn't notice.

"Are you coming?" she said to her little sister.

"Why don't you stay for a little while, Lisa?" Dr. Emily said. "I'm sure Mandy would like that."

Mandy looked at her mother gratefully. "Grandma and Grandpa are coming," she said to Lisa. "Grandma is bringing some of the doughnuts she made."

Lisa tried to smile, but it was a real effort for her.

"That would be nice," she said. "Can I stay here with Carla for a little while?"

Dr. Emily nodded. "Of course you can," she said. "I'll show you what we do to get rid of mites."

Jennifer shuddered again. "Better you than

me," she said. "Don't be home late, Lisa. I'll tell Mom you're staying for a while."

Mandy watched as Jennifer closed the clinic door behind her. "Some people!" she said.

"Now, now, Mandy," Dr. Emily said. "Not everybody is prepared for the work that goes into keeping a pet. At least Jennifer realizes she hasn't done very well."

"Hmmph!" said Mandy. Then she looked at Lisa.

Lisa was bending over Carla, stroking her shabby fur, talking to her.

"At least I can talk to her and play with her — until she goes to a new home," Lisa said.

Dr. Emily smiled. "I've got an idea about that," she said.

"Oh, Mom, what?" said Mandy.

Dr. Emily shook her head. "Let's get Carla better first," she said. "That's the most important thing."

Mandy nodded her head. "Of course it is," she agreed.

"Lisa, would you like to help?" Dr. Emily asked. "Or perhaps you don't like mites either."

Lisa picked Carla up and cuddled her. "I *don't* like mites," she replied. "Not when they make Carla scratch all her fur off. But that doesn't mean I won't touch Carla. Of course I want to help."

Dr. Emily smiled. "There you are," she said. "I knew it!"

"What?" asked Mandy.

"Lisa is a born pet lover," Dr. Emily said. "I think we're going to have to think of a very special home for Carla!"

5

A Good Idea!

"So, how do we get rid of these mites?" Mandy asked.

"We have to bathe the guinea pig in this," Dr. Emily said, taking a bottle down from a shelf and putting it on the counter.

She ran warm water into a bowl while Mandy looked at the liquid in the bottle.

"What does this do?" asked Lisa.

"It kills the mites," said Dr. Emily. "If we don't get rid of them Carla would get very sick indeed."

"You mean she might die?" Lisa said.

Dr. Emily nodded. She picked up the bottle and carefully measured a small amount of liquid into a dish. Then she poured it into the bowl of water.

"Mandy, you get a fresh towel, and, Lisa, you hand Carla to me when I ask for her."

Dr. Emily put on a pair of fine rubber gloves, swirled the mixture in the bowl around to mix it thoroughly and held out her hands for Carla.

Lisa placed the little guinea pig carefully into Dr. Emily's hands.

"We have to make sure the mixture soaks right down into her skin," explained Dr. Emily. "It won't work otherwise."

"And what then?" asked Lisa.

"Then we wait for two weeks," said Dr. Emily. "We might have to do this again. But with any luck one treatment should do the trick."

Mandy and Lisa watched as Dr. Emily scooped the solution over Carla, being careful to cover all her fur. Carla didn't mind at all. She seemed to really like the warm water.

"There," said Dr. Emily at last. "I think that's enough. Ready with that towel, Mandy?"

Mandy spread the fluffy white towel out on the examination table and Dr. Emily placed Carla in the middle of it.

"Now what?" asked Mandy.

"Lisa, wrap the towel around Carla and let her dry naturally," Dr. Emily said. "And that's it."

"You mean she'll get better now?" said Lisa.

"I hope so," said Dr. Emily.

Mandy watched as Lisa wrapped the little animal up in the soft towel. Dr. Emily was also watching Lisa. Lisa was so gentle with Carla.

"Isn't it awful that Lisa is going to lose Carla?" Mandy said to her mom. "Couldn't we keep her here until she's better? Then maybe Jennifer would take her back — once Carla looks nice again."

Dr. Emily smiled. "You know the rules, Mandy," she said. "If we kept all the animals you wanted us to keep, we'd have no room for patients!"

Mandy nodded. She knew what her mom said made sense.

Lisa looked up. "At least I can look after her today," she said. "And maybe I can see her before she goes to her new home. Jennifer never let me do this before."

Lisa stood with Carla wrapped up in the towel in her arms. There were tears in her eyes. She really was going to miss Carla.

"What if we sent her to people who would let you come and visit?" Dr. Emily suggested.

"That would be wonderful," Lisa said.

"And what if these people let you try to get Carla back into condition?" said Dr. Emily.

"You mean so that Jennifer would take her back?" said Lisa.

Dr. Emily put her head on one side. "Jennifer has a lot to learn about looking after pets," she said. "Pets don't win prizes if they aren't well looked after."

"I would *love* to look after Carla," Lisa said.

"*I* would like Jennifer to see what a difference taking care of a pet makes," Dr. Emily said. "And to see that if you want your pet to win a prize, *somebody* has to look after it."

"You mean Lisa," said Mandy.

"I think Lisa would make a wonderful nurse

for Carla," Dr. Emily said. "Much better than Jennifer."

"If we can get Carla back into condition then Jennifer might even want to put her into the show," said Lisa. "But she still won't like looking after her."

"But she might let *you* look after her," said Mandy.

Dr. Emily nodded. "That's what I was thinking," she said. "That way, everybody would be happy. Jennifer would have her prizewinning guinea pig and Lisa would be able to take care of Carla."

"Oh, that would be wonderful, Dr. Emily," Lisa said eagerly. Then she looked doubtful. "But what about Mom? She's made up her mind that Carla has to go. I don't think she would trust me to look after Carla — not after all that trouble with Jennifer."

Dr. Emily smiled. "Well, *I* think you'd be very good at looking after a pet, Lisa," she said. "But we'd have to prove that to Jennifer — and to your mom."

"It's worth a try," said Mandy.

"But I can't take her home," said Lisa. "So where is she going to live?"

Dr. Emily's eyes twinkled. "Who's coming?" she said, teasing.

Mandy's mouth dropped open. "Grandma and Grandpa," she said. "They'll do it. I'm sure they will. Mom, you're brilliant!"

Lisa looked at Mandy and Dr. Emily. "You mean they'll look after Carla for me? They'll let me come and visit?"

"Of course they will," Mandy said. "All we have to do is ask them!"

6

Carla's New Home

"A guinea pig?" Grandpa said as they sat around the kitchen table at Animal Ark munching doughnuts. "We've never had a guinea pig before."

"You'll love Carla," Mandy said. "Lisa and I will take you to visit her in a minute. She's beautiful."

"She doesn't look her best at the moment," Lisa explained. "But usually she does look beautiful."

"I'm sure she does," Grandma said, smiling at Lisa. "And we'll be glad to keep her for you for a few weeks."

"There now," Dr. Emily said. "Grandma and Grandpa to the rescue!"

"We'll come over to Lilac Cottage every day to see Carla," Mandy said.

"We'll clean out her cage and feed her and everything," Lisa promised. "She won't be any trouble, honestly."

"But what are you going to say to Jennifer?" Grandma said. "Won't she want to know where Carla has gone?"

"We can tell her the truth," said Mandy. "We can say you and Grandpa are looking after Carla. But we don't have to tell her our plan."

"I suppose not," Grandma said. "After all, Carla will be well taken care of, and that's the important thing."

"Exactly," said Mandy.

"You'll have to give us a few lessons in looking after guinea pigs though," Grandpa said.

Lisa nodded. "I've got a book at home. I'll lend it to you."

"When do you think Carla will be ready to go to her new home, Mom?" Mandy asked.

Dr. Emily smiled. "I think she should be ready tomorrow evening," she said. "But I'd like to make sure her treatment is working before I send her off."

"She'll need careful grooming for a few weeks," Dr. Adam added.

"But her coat will grow back, won't it?" asked Lisa.

Dr. Adam nodded. "Of course it will," he said. "It might not be as perfect as it was before, but there's no reason she shouldn't make a full recovery."

"I'll buy a baby hairbrush," Lisa said. "The Guinea Pig Gang told me that would be good to use for grooming. Oh, it's so wonderful to have the chance to look after Carla."

Lisa's eyes were shining with happiness.

"Thanks, Grandma," Mandy whispered. "Thanks a lot!"

Lisa jumped up. "Do you want to see Carla now?" she said to Mandy's grandma and grandpa.

Grandma smiled. "Of course!" she said.

Grandpa got up from his chair. Lisa was already halfway to the door, eager to show Carla off.

"If she's going to come and live with us we'll have to introduce ourselves," he said. "Do you think she'll like us?"

Lisa nodded her head as she swung the kitchen door open. "Come and see," she said. "Carla will love you. I just know she will!"

Mandy, Lisa, and James stopped off at the general store on the way home from school next day.

"Mrs. McFarlane sells everything," James said as they pushed open the general store's door. "She's bound to have a baby hairbrush."

"A hairbrush!" said a voice. "You certainly

look as if you could do with a hairbrush, James Hunter. Your hair is falling into your eyes."

James shoved his hair away from his eyes and his glasses slipped down his nose.

"Hello, Mrs. Ponsonby," Mandy said. "How is Pandora?"

Mrs. Ponsonby was a large, bossy woman with pink glasses. She was wearing a bright blue hat with a feather in it and carrying a Pekingese under her arm.

"She's very well," Mrs. Ponsonby said, and Mandy tickled the little dog under the chin. "What do you want a hairbrush for?"

It was no use trying to avoid Mrs. Ponsonby or her questions. It was easier just to answer them.

"It's for a guinea pig," Mandy said. "A baby's hairbrush is good for grooming."

"Really?" said Mrs. Ponsonby. "I wonder if I should try that with my Pandora."

"I've got some baby hairbrushes here some-where," said Mrs. McFarlane from behind the counter. "Now where did I see them?"

Mandy grinned. Mrs. McFarlane's shop was like Aladdin's cave. The shelves were full to overflowing with all sorts of things. It was Mandy and James's favorite shop in the village.

"There they are," said James, pointing to a box on the top shelf near the door.

"Now what are they doing up there?" Mrs. McFarlane said. "I'll just get the stepladder."

Mrs. McFarlane bustled off into the back of the shop.

"Oh, look!" said Lisa. "There's a notice about the Welford Show." She read it eagerly. "There it is — there's the guinea pig competition," she said.

"So it's *your* guinea pig you want the hairbrush for," Mrs. Ponsonby said to Lisa.

Lisa bit her lip. "Not exactly," she said.

Mrs. Ponsonby looked suspicious.

"It's really my sister Jennifer's guinea pig," Lisa said. "But Mandy's grandma and grandpa are going to look after it for a little while and I'm going to help them."

Mrs. Ponsonby looked puzzled, but Mrs.

McFarlane came back with the stepladder at that moment and set it up next to the shelves.

"You can get down one of those hairbrushes for me, too," Mrs. Ponsonby said. "That pink one looks nice."

Mrs. McFarlane was halfway up the stepladder. "This one?" she said, pointing to a pale pink one.

Mrs. Ponsonby put Pandora down on the floor and pointed again. "No, no," she said. "That nice *bright* pink one."

Pandora scampered over to the ladder and tried to jump up on the first step.

"Now, then, sweetums," Mrs. Ponsonby said to the Pekingese. "Don't be naughty. Come back."

Pandora looked around and barked. She hopped up on the first step of the ladder just as Mrs. Ponsonby made a lunge for her.

"Whoops," said Mrs. Ponsonby as she missed Pandora and bumped into the ladder. Her hat fell down over her eyes, the feather waving wildly.

"Watch out!" Lisa called as the ladder wobbled.

James made a dive for the ladder and grabbed it. "Hold on," he shouted.

Mrs. McFarlane clutched the ladder tightly. Pandora barked and sprang off the step, wrapping her leash around James's ankles. The ladder began to wobble again.

"Help, Mandy!" James called.

Mandy leaped to the ladder and clutched at it. Mrs. McFarlane hung on.

"Be careful, James," Mrs. Ponsonby shouted. "Make sure you don't stand on my poor Pandora."

Pandora wrapped her leash even tighter around James's ankles. He looked at Mandy and made a face.

"It's all right, Mrs. Ponsonby. I couldn't move even if I wanted to," James said.

Mrs. Ponsonby scooped Pandora up. She yanked the leash free of James's legs — he lost his balance and sat down suddenly on the floor.

"Really! You children!" Mrs. Ponsonby said,

shaking her head. "Poor Pandora is scared out of her wits."

Pandora struggled to get down again, but Mrs. Ponsonby held on to her. The little dog didn't look in the least bit scared.

"Us?" said James. "It wasn't *our* fault."

Mandy clutched the ladder tightly. "Are you all right, Mrs. McFarlane?"

Mrs. McFarlane looked down at them. "If you ask me, I think I'm in the safest place," she said. "Now, what about these hairbrushes? What color do you want, Lisa?"

Lisa was shaking with laughter. "Oh, pink!" she said. "Make mine pink, too."

"I think I'll bring the whole box down," Mrs. McFarlane suggested. "It'll be safer."

Mandy, James, and Lisa watched as Mrs. Ponsonby paid for her hairbrush and magazines and sailed out of the shop.

"She didn't even apologize," Lisa said.

Mandy grinned. "Mrs. Ponsonby *never* apologizes."

"That's because Mrs. Ponsonby is never

wrong," Mrs. McFarlane added, and winked.

"Come on," said James, dusting himself down. "Let's go and see if Carla is ready to go to her new home!"

Carla *was* ready.

"She seems fine," Dr. Emily said. "She hasn't been scratching at all today. But I'll still need to see her in two weeks to make sure."

"So can we take her to Grandma and Grandpa's?" Mandy asked.

Dr. Emily nodded. "Tell Grandma to keep her away from drafts as much as possible. Poor Carla will be a bit cold until her coat grows again."

Mandy and James put Carla's feed and hay in plastic bags and Lisa picked up the cage.

"Ready?" she said to the other two.

"Ready!" said Mandy and James.

"Hi, Grandma! Hi Grandpa!" Mandy called as they pushed open the gate at Lilac Cottage. "We've brought your visitor."

Grandma and Grandpa came to the door and looked at the cage Lisa was holding.

"My, my," Grandma said. "She looks better already."

"Do you think so?" Lisa asked, as she and Mandy came up the garden path.

Grandpa nodded. "She looks a lot better than she did last night," he said. "She's as bright as a button."

"Come on in and let's get her settled down," said Grandma.

Lisa carried Carla into the kitchen.

"I thought we would keep her in the utility room," Grandma said, leading them into a little room off the kitchen. "It's nice and warm in here."

"It's perfect," said Lisa, setting the cage down on the worktable.

"This is great," said Mandy. "Mom and Dad said to keep her out of drafts. She'll be really cozy in here."

"She seems happy enough already," Grandma

said to Lisa with a smile. "Look! She's made herself right at home."

Lisa looked at Carla. The little guinea pig settled down on her haunches and began to clean her whiskers.

"Oh, Carla," Lisa said. "I think you're going to like your new home a lot."

"Now," said Grandpa. "You'd better give us our first lesson. We've got a lot to learn about guinea pigs."

Lisa filled Carla's water bottle and fixed it to the bars of her cage.

"She needs lots of fresh water," she said. "Guinea pigs get thirsty just like us."

"I'm glad you mentioned that," said Grandpa. "How about something to drink while we're having our lesson?"

"And cookies?" added Mandy.

"Of course," Grandma said.

Mandy smiled. Carla was going to be well looked after. And maybe, soon, she would be back at home with Lisa. Mandy crossed her fingers. Their plan just *had* to work!

7

Bad News

Carla's coat soon began to grow again. Lisa visited Lilac Cottage every day to play with Carla and to groom her. Most days Mandy and James went along, too.

Sometimes Pam brought Ginny to play with Carla.

"Oh, look at them," said Lisa one evening at Grandma's. "They're so happy together."

The two guinea pigs were chasing each other around the backyard. Grandpa had made a run for Carla so that she could have some exercise every day.

"Carla's coat is nearly back to normal," Pam said.

Mandy nodded happily. "Mom checked her last week," she said. "The mites are all gone and Mom thinks Carla is going to make a com-

plete recovery. Her coat is going to be just as beautiful as ever."

"She's certainly a much happier little guinea pig than when I *first* saw her," Grandma said, looking at the two little animals scampering around the grass and tumbling over each other. "It's lovely to see her playing like that. You're right, Pam. Guinea pigs do like company."

"Maybe it's time Carla joined the Guinea Pig Gang," Pam said.

Lisa's eyes lit up. "What a good idea," she said. "I'm sure Carla would love that."

"Why don't you have your next meeting here?" Grandma suggested.

"Terrific," said Pam. "I'll let the gang know. Is it all right if we come this Friday?"

Grandma nodded. "I'll make some of my extra-special cookies," she said.

The Guinea Pig Gang assembled at Lilac Cottage right on time. The only person missing was Lisa. Mandy frowned. It wasn't like Lisa to be late — not when she was coming to visit Carla.

"There's going to be a special section for pedigree guinea pigs," Ross was saying. "There are people coming from all over the place to show their guinea pigs."

Mandy smiled. She was really looking forward to the Welford Show and so were the rest of the Guinea Pig Gang. They were all going to see the guinea pig competition and cheer Carla on.

"Here comes Lisa," said James.

"Hi!" Mandy called.

Lisa raised her hand and waved, but she looked very worried.

"What's wrong?" asked Mandy.

Lisa bit her lip. "Mom has been talking to Mrs. Ponsonby," she said.

"What about?" asked James.

"About Carla," Lisa said. "Mrs. Ponsonby told Mom that she had seen me buying a hairbrush for my guinea pig. So I had to tell Mom all about visiting Carla at Lilac Cottage. I told her Carla was doing so well Jennifer would want to take her back and put her in the show after all."

"That's just like Mrs. Ponsonby," James said. "Interfering again!"

"What did your mom say?" asked Mandy.

"She says Jennifer can't have Carla back," Lisa said. "She says it isn't fair to Carla."

"Didn't you tell her you would look after Carla?" Pam asked.

Lisa nodded. "Mom said if Jennifer couldn't look after a guinea pig then neither can I. She says I'm too young."

"But that isn't true," said Mandy. "You do such a good job of taking care of Carla. Why don't you ask your mom to come and see Carla? Then she'll see how well you can look after her."

Lisa shook her head. "She says your grandma and grandpa are looking after her, not me."

"But *you* taught *us* how to look after her," Grandma said.

"It's no good," said Lisa. "Jennifer complained so much about Carla, it made Mom change her mind about having a pet."

"That isn't fair," said Pam. "You're great with Carla."

"Thanks," said Lisa. "But there's no point in Jennifer putting Carla in the show now."

"What a pity," said Pam. "I'm entering Ginny in the pet guinea pig competition. In fact the Guinea Pig Gang are all entering their pets. I thought we could all go to the show together."

Mandy's face lit up. "*I* know!" she said. "Why don't *you* enter Carla in the pedigree section, Lisa? And if she wins a prize, your mom will see how well you've looked after her."

Lisa shook her head. "Mom isn't going to the show."

"But she's just *got* to see her," said Pam.

"How?" Mandy asked. "We can't drag her to Lilac Cottage."

"No, but we could take Carla to see *her*," James suggested.

Lisa shrugged. "It wouldn't do any good," she said. "Mom says Carla deserves a home with somebody who is old enough to look after her properly."

Grandma appeared at the kitchen door.

"Oh, Grandma, did you hear that?" Mandy said anxiously. "Lisa's mom won't have Carla back."

"Hold on," said Grandma. "Calm down and start at the beginning. I'm sure things aren't as bad as they seem."

Mandy took a deep breath. Maybe Grandma was right. There had to be a way to solve the problem.

Mandy explained and Grandma looked thoughtful. Mandy waited, hardly daring to breathe.

"How many weeks is it until the show?" Grandma asked.

"Two," James replied.

"Well," Grandma said slowly, "that isn't very long. I'll have to get a move on if I'm going to get all that baking done in time. And I'll need some help with the booth."

Mandy looked at her grandma. Her heart sank. Baking! What about Carla? Surely Grandma wasn't more interested in her booth at the show?

Grandma smiled at Lisa. "Do you think your mom would help me with my booth if I asked her?"

"Of course she would," Lisa said.

"So she *would* be at the show after all," James said, catching on to Grandma's idea.

Mandy let her breath out. "And then you could make sure she saw Carla. Grandma, you're so clever!"

Lisa still looked a little doubtful.

"It'll work," said James reassuringly.

"*If* Carla wins a prize," Lisa said. "Oh, I hope she does."

"She will," said Mandy. "Of course she will!"

8

The Welford Show

Grandma and Grandpa had already arrived at the Welford Show when Mandy and James got there. Mandy looked around the church field where the show took place every year.

There were tents set up here and there for the booths. There were lots of games and rides. There was even a greased pole. Mandy saw Peter Foster trying to climb it. He was nearly at the top. Timmy was running around the bottom of the pole, barking his head off.

The field was crowded with people — all of Welford seemed to be there. This was going to be the best show ever!

"He's nearly made it," said James, watching Peter.

As they watched, Peter reached for the top — and his hand slipped. He came sliding all the way down to the bottom. Timmy started to leap up at him while Peter tried to brush him off.

"Peter looks as if he needs a bath," said Dr. Adam, laughing.

"And so does Timmy — now!" Mandy said.

"There's Grandma's booth," Dr. Emily said, pointing to a tent at the edge of the field. "Why don't you go and say hello, Mandy?"

Mandy was looking around, her eyes glowing with excitement. She could see Laura Baker with her rabbits, Fluffy, Nibbles, and Patch. Richard Tanner had Duchess safely in her cat basket and Gary had Gertie draped around his neck.

"Look at all the pets," she said. "Isn't it great?"

Dr. Adam and Dr. Emily laughed. "There are enough here to satisfy even you, Mandy," Dr. Adam said.

"Come on," James said to Mandy. "Let's go and ask your grandma where Lisa and Carla are. I don't see them, do you?"

Mandy dragged her eyes away from a cage with two adorable black-and-white kittens in it.

"Lisa was coming with her mom and Jennifer," Mandy said. "Grandma and Grandpa were bringing Carla."

Mandy and James made their way to Grandma's booth. Mrs. Glover was arranging cakes on a plate and Grandma was unpacking more goodies from plastic boxes.

"Hi, Grandma. Hi, Mrs. Glover," Mandy said.

"Hello, you two," Mrs. Glover said. "Are you

entering Blackie in one of the competitions, James?"

James looked at Blackie and shook his head. "Not this year," he said. "Blackie is too young."

"Next year then," Mrs. Glover said. "Blackie is an adorable puppy. He looks like a prize-winner to me."

James looked thoughtful. "Maybe," he said. "But only the very best pets win prizes."

"That's right," Mandy said quickly. "A pet has got to be really special to win."

"And well taken care of," Mrs. Glover said. "Keeping a pet is a big responsibility."

"But if you really love animals then you *like* looking after them," Mandy said.

Mrs. Glover looked thoughtful. "I suppose you do," she said. "Lisa is very fond of animals, but she's too young to have a pet."

"Lisa is the same age as me," James pointed out.

"Is she?" said Mrs. Glover, looking even more thoughtful. "Your grandma has been telling me how good Lisa is with Carla, Mandy."

"Oh, she is," said Mandy. "You'd be surprised, Mrs. Glover."

Out of the corner of her eye, Mandy saw Grandma wink at her.

"Lisa is looking for you," said Grandma. "I think she has something to show you."

"Where is she?" James asked.

Grandma nodded toward a group of children gathered in a corner of the field.

"The Guinea Pig Gang," Mandy said. "See you later, Grandma. Bye, Mrs. Glover."

Mandy and James made their way toward the Guinea Pig Gang. Lisa was right in the middle of it — with Carla.

Mandy put a finger through the bars of Carla's cage and the little animal sniffed it.

"She's looking great," Mandy said. "Her coat is just as nice as ever."

"Does your mom know Carla is here?" James asked Lisa.

Lisa shook her head. Her eyes were bright with excitement. "Mandy's grandpa smuggled her in," she said. "I thought I would keep her out of Mom's way until the competition."

"Good thinking," Mandy said. "After all, we don't want to spoil the surprise, do we?"

Lisa smiled nervously. "I hope it works," she said, looking at Carla.

James smiled. "Mandy's grandma has been telling your mom how good you are at looking after Carla," he said.

"I think your mom might be starting to change her mind already," said Mandy. "Just wait till she sees Carla."

"We'd still have to persuade Jennifer to take Carla back," Lisa said.

"Oh, that won't be a problem," Mandy said. "Not once Carla has won a prize!"

"And now for the pedigree guinea pig competition," the announcer said. "Would all the owners please bring their guinea pigs forward to the judges' table?"

Lisa looked at Mandy and James. "Wish me luck," she said.

Mandy gave her a thumbs-up sign but James was looking around.

"Where's Jennifer?" he asked.

Mandy looked around, too. Grandma was walking toward them with Mrs. Glover at her side. Mrs. Glover looked slightly puzzled. But there was no sign of Jennifer.

"We'll find her," Mandy said. "Good luck, Lisa!"

Mandy and James watched Lisa move forward with Carla in her cage. There were five other purebred guinea pigs in the competition — a black-and-white Dutch, two rosetted Abyssinians, a self golden, and a beautiful white Himalayan with brown-gray markings. Carla was up against very stiff competition indeed.

"Come on," urged James. "We don't have much time."

Mandy raced after him, in and out of the crowd, searching furiously. Jennifer was nowhere to be seen.

"She must be around somewhere," said Mandy.

"There she is," James said, pointing to a group of girls in the corner.

"Jennifer!" Mandy called.

Jennifer looked around and frowned. "What is it?" she asked, coming over to them.

"We want to show you something," James said.

"What?" said Jennifer.

"Just come with us — please, Jennifer," Mandy pleaded.

Jennifer shrugged her shoulders. "All right, but it had better be worth it."

Mandy and James almost dragged her over to the pedigree guinea pig competition.

"I'm not interested in guinea pigs anymore," Jennifer said when she saw where they were going.

"But you *will* be," said James. "Wait and see."

Mandy made her way through the crowds to the front of the judges' table. The chief judge was just taking Carla out of her cage.

"Look," Mandy said. "It's Carla."

Jennifer's mouth dropped open. "Carla!" she said. "It can't be. Her coat was a mess."

"It isn't any longer," James said. "Lisa has been looking after her."

"Lisa?" said Jennifer.

"Shh," Mandy said. "They're going to announce the winner."

Mandy hardly dared to breathe as the chief judge stood up. Lisa was standing in front of Carla's cage, her eyes round with excitement.

"We've got an exceptionally fine collection of guinea pigs here," the judge said. "But there

can be only one winner." He paused and
Mandy swallowed hard.

"Carla," James whispered.

"Abby, the Abyssinian," the judge said.

"Oh, no," Mandy said. "Poor Lisa!"

Lisa was still standing in front of the judges'
table. She bit her lip, holding back the tears.
Then, as the judge awarded the rosette to the
Abyssinian guinea pig, Lisa picked up Carla's
cage, turned away, and walked toward them.

Mandy tried to smile, but it was impossible.
Then she saw her grandma and Mrs. Glover

making their way through the crowd toward them.

"It's all right, Lisa," James said as Lisa came up. "You did your best and so did Carla."

Lisa looked miserably at them both. Then she looked at Jennifer.

"I didn't know you were entering Carla in this competition," Jennifer said.

Lisa looked down at Carla. "I'm sorry, Jennifer," she said. "I suppose I should have asked you, but I didn't think you'd let me do it."

"I wouldn't have," Jennifer said, staring at Carla. "I can't believe my eyes. Look at Carla's coat!"

A tall man, one of the judges, passed by and heard her.

"Make sure you enter Carla next year," he said to Lisa. He looked at the others. "Lisa told me about the mites," he went on. "I'm afraid Carla's coat hasn't quite recovered. If it had, she definitely would have won. I've never seen such a fine tort and white. Somebody has obviously taken very good care of her." He smiled at Lisa and walked on.

"Well," Mrs. Glover said to Lisa. "I certainly am surprised. Mandy's grandma told me you had taken good care of Carla, but I didn't real- ize just how well you had looked after her, Lisa."

Lisa tried to smile as she handed Carla's cage to Grandma. "Would you mind keeping her until we find a good home for her?" she said.

"You can't give her away now," said Jennifer.

Lisa spun round in surprise. "Well, *you* don't want her. That's why I entered her in the com- petition. I thought you might want to take her back if she won a prize."

"Is *that* why you did all this?" Jennifer asked softly.

Lisa nodded, hardly able to speak. "I thought she could win prizes for you and I could do all the work of looking after her. I love looking after her."

Jennifer looked at her mother. "Oh, Mom," she said. "We can't let Carla go — not now. I'm sorry I didn't take good care of her. Lisa was right all along. I should have let her share Carla."

"Are you saying you would look after Carla now?" Mrs. Glover asked.

Jennifer shook her head. "Not me," she said. "You were right. Pets need people who *really* love them. I'm not a pet person."

"But *I* am," said Lisa eagerly. "Oh, Mom, can I take care of Carla? I promise I'll look after her — honestly."

Mrs. Glover looked from Jennifer to Lisa. "I don't know —" she began.

"Lisa *can* look after Carla, Mom," Jennifer said. "She's proved it. And she's taught me a lesson."

"I'm certainly glad you've learned your lesson about pets, Jennifer," Mrs. Glover said.

Grandma gave a little cough and Mrs. Glover looked at her. "What do you think, Dorothy?"

Grandma smiled. "I don't think Carla could have a better owner than Lisa," she said.

"I agree," Jennifer said. "Lisa *deserves* to have Carla for her pet."

Mrs. Glover looked at Lisa and Carla. "It's your birthday soon, Lisa," she said.

Lisa looked puzzled. "Yes," she said. "In two weeks."

"I think Jennifer is right," Mrs. Glover said, smiling. "I'll tell you what. Jennifer can have a stereo after all, and Lisa, you can have Carla for your birthday. How's that?"

"Great!" said Jennifer.

"Perfect!" Lisa said, then turned to Mandy and James. "Did you hear that? I can have Carla for my very own."

Just then Pam Stanton came rushing up. "Guess what?" she said. "Ginny won the pet guinea pig competition. The Guinea Pig Gang are going to celebrate, and you and Carla are invited, Lisa."

Pam rushed off again and Lisa watched her go. "You know," she said, "I don't care if Carla *never* wins a prize — just so long as she's *my* guinea pig."

Mandy and James smiled at her.

"Do you think we're invited to the Guinea Pig Gang's celebration as well?" James asked.

"Of course you are," Lisa said. "You're honorary members."

"And you're a real member now," said Mandy.

Lisa grinned. "Did you hear that, Carla?" she said. "We're full-fledged members of the Guinea Pig Gang — both of us!"